TRIPLET TROUBLE
and
the Runaway Reindeer

TRIPLET TROUBLE
and
the Runaway Reindeer

by Debbie Dadey and Marcia Thornton Jones
Illustrated by John Speirs

A
LITTLE APPLE
PAPERBACK

SCHOLASTIC INC.
New York Toronto London Auckland Sydney

ISBN 0-590-25473-1

Text copyright © 1995 by Marcia Thornton Jones and Debra S. Dadey.
Illustrations copyright © 1995 by Scholastic Inc.
All rights reserved. Published by Scholastic Inc.
APPLE PAPERBACKS is a registered trademark of Scholastic Inc.

12 11 10 9 8 7 6 5 4 3 2 1   5 6 7 8 9/9 0/0

Printed in the U.S.A.   40

First Scholastic printing, November 1995

*For Dasher, Dancer, Prancer, Vixen,
Comet, Cupid, Donder, Blitzen, and
especially Rudolph*

Contents

TRIPLET TROUBLE
and
the Runaway Reindeer

Secret Santas

The whole second-grade class clapped when Mr. Parker held up a sign. In big red letters it said: SECRET SANTA DAY.

Usually when Mr. Parker held up a sign it meant more work, but not today.

I couldn't wait to tell my best friend Alex Tucker that I, Sam Johnson, was the one who had been leaving her little presents all week.

"Who would like to go first?" Mr. Parker asked.

I was the first one to raise my hand so Mr. Parker nodded at me.

I dropped a candy bar on Alex's desk.

"Merry Christmas from your Secret Santa," I said.

Alex smiled. She had a space where her tooth used to be. "You're the best Secret Santa I've ever had. Thanks!" Alex ate the candy bar in three bites.

"Sam can't be Alex's Santa," Barbara complained. "*I'm* her Secret Santa!"

Maria stood up and shook her head. "That's not right. I'm Alex's Secret Santa."

Everyone in the room looked at Alex. Her blond hair stuck out in crazy directions. She had peppermint candies tied to the ends of twenty tiny ponytails. Alex is a triplet. She is always thinking up ways to be different from her brother and sister. Usually, her ideas get her in trouble.

Mr. Parker rubbed his chin. "Alex," he asked, "do you know why you have so many Secret Santas?"

"Maybe I put my name in the hat too many times?" she said.

"That's cheating!" Ashley Tucker called out. Ashley is Alex's sister. She always wants everything perfect.

Adam Tucker waved his hand in the air. Adam is Alex's brother and very smart.

"That means some people didn't have a Secret Santa at all," Adam said.

I looked at Alex and frowned. Now I knew why I didn't get a single present all week.

"Alex should be punished," Barbara called out. "She ruined everything."

I nodded my head. Alex Tucker had done a terrible thing.

2

The Contest

Mr. Parker made Alex write a letter to the class. She had to read it in the front of the room. Alex said that she learned her lesson and she felt bad. I decided to make sure she felt bad.

"Sam?" Alex asked at recess. "Do you want to have a snowball fight?"

I pulled my wool hat down over my ears.

I pretended not to hear. But Alex didn't give up. "Sam? Want to play chase?"

I looked at Alex. She wore one red mitten and one purple glove. Her right boot was red and the left boot was yellow.

"Leave me alone," I yelled at her. "If it wasn't for you, I would have gotten a Secret Santa present."

Alex put her head down and walked away. I felt bad. But just for a minute. After all, I wasn't the one who cheated. I ran to Ashley and Adam. We had fun making a snowman until the bell rang.

After recess Mr. Parker held up another sign. This sign wasn't one that he had written. It had big gold letters on bright red paper. It said:

HOLIDAY HOUSE DECORATING CONTEST. PRIZE: TOYS FROM THELMA'S TOY TRUNK.

"Wow!" The whole class cheered. Thelma's Toy Trunk was the biggest toy store in town.

9

"The prize goes to the best-decorated house in the neighborhood!" Mr. Parker said. "Remember, fair play only!" He looked at Alex.

I looked at Alex, too. Her eyes got real big. Then she snapped her fingers right in front of her nose. That could only mean one thing. Alex had an idea.

3

Twinkling Lights

"I thought you were going to help us," I said to Alex. It was after school and Ashley, Adam, and I were decorating for the contest.

"I will," Alex said, "but first, let's play in the snow." Alex twirled around, trying to catch snowflakes on her tongue. All she got was dizzy. She flopped down on the ground and waved her arms and legs in big arches. I figured that was as close to an angel as Alex would ever get.

"We can't play," Adam said. "We have to help Sam decorate for the contest."

"Then he'll help us," Ashley added.

"It was your idea, so why aren't you helping?" I asked.

Alex rolled across the yard, trying to turn herself into a snowman. My dog Cleo chased her. Cleo jumped on Alex to lick all the snowflakes off her cheeks. Alex laughed and threw a snowball for Cleo to catch.

"Don't you want to win the toys from Thelma's Toy Trunk?" Adam asked.

Alex jumped up. "They have the best toys," she said.

"That's why I want to win," I told her.

"The winning decorations have to be special," Alex said. "Something really different." Alex's hair still stuck out in peppermint ponytails.

"Most people just use regular Christmas decorations," I said. "Like plastic Santas and twinkling lights."

I held out a knotted string of lights. Cleo jumped up and grabbed them from my hand. That's when Alex's eyes got real big. She snapped her fingers right in front of her nose.

Santa Scene

Funny noises woke me up the next morning. Something was happening at the Tuckers' house.

I ran to the triplets' house. Cleo jumped through the snow after me as we passed the four houses between mine and the Tuckers'.

Alex, Adam, and Ashley were in the

front yard. All three were wearing red Santa hats. They were trying to get their scarecrow from last Halloween to stand up straight.

"What are you doing?" I asked.

"Decorating!" Adam said with a grin.

Ashley nodded. "We're going to win those toys."

"But you haven't finished helping me!" I said.

Alex shrugged. "Don't worry, we'll get something for you when we win."

I looked at the lopsided scarecrow. "That doesn't look like a winning Christmas decoration to me," I told the triplets.

"We're not done yet," Alex said. "Just wait! I have it all planned."

I sat down on the front step of their porch to watch.

Adam dressed the scarecrow in long red underwear, stuffing the shirt with an old blanket to make it look fat.

Ashley made a family of snowmen. She gave each one a candy cane to hold.

Alex painted a fireplace on the back of her science fair poster. She propped it behind Ashley's snowman family.

Finally, the three Tuckers pulled their old wagon from the garage and put it in front of their Santa Claus scarecrow. Adam tied a broom and mop to the bottom of the wagon while Ashley and Alex taped a huge box to the sides. They all stood back and smiled.

"How do you like it?" Alex asked me.

"What is it?" I finally asked.

Alex grinned. "It's the Tucker Triplet Christmas scene!" she said proudly. "Complete with Santa and his sled, a snowman family, and a fireplace!"

I looked at the Tucker yard and shook my head. It didn't look like a Christmas scene to me. The smile melted from Adam's face.

"If Sam can't tell what it is, the judges won't know, either," Adam said. "We don't stand a chance of winning the contest."

Ashley looked ready to cry. "We should have known better than to listen to one of Alex's ideas. The yard looks stupid!"

I like Ashley, and I like Adam. But when they gang up on Alex there's trouble. Triplet trouble.

Red Nose

"Wait here!" Alex yelled. "I have another idea." She raced into the house. In a few minutes she came out with big brown paper bags, string, and scissors.

"What are you doing?" Adam asked.

"Wait," Alex said. "I'm building something special that will help us win."

Adam, Ashley, and I watched as Alex

23

cut and cut. Finally, Alex held up something that looked like two dead trees.

Alex smiled at Cleo, my dog. I didn't like the way Alex smiled. Cleo whined.

Before I could stop her Alex grabbed Cleo.

"Why are you putting dead trees on my dog's head?" I asked Alex.

"They're antlers," Alex told me. "They make Cleo special."

"A special what?" Ashley asked.

"A special reindeer!" Alex yelled.

"No way!" Adam said.

Ashley took the red bow off her head and tied it around Cleo's neck. Then she sneezed and stood back. Ashley always sneezed around Cleo. "How sweet!" she said.

"This isn't such a good idea," Adam told Alex.

"You're right," Alex said. "I forgot something." She pulled a big red paper dot out of her pocket. Alex stuck the dot right on Cleo's nose.

Ashley sneezed again and giggled. "Cleo looks cute, even if she does make me sneeze."

"Cleo is not cute," I said. "She's my dog and she's special enough without antlers. I don't want her to be a reindeer."

Cleo whined and scratched at the red dot nose. I could tell she didn't want to be a reindeer.

Alex stuck out her lip. "You're just mad because you didn't think of it first."

I looked at Alex. Then I looked at Cleo. Cleo was busy trying to knock the antlers off with her front paws.

Alex put her arm around me. "Don't worry, Sam. I'll take good care of Cleo. Being a reindeer won't hurt her one bit."

I stared at Alex. For some reason, I was *very* worried about Cleo.

Missing

I was right to be worried. The next morning Cleo was missing.

"Cleo!" I yelled out the back door. Nothing. No Cleo.

"Cleo!" I yelled out the front door. Nothing. No Cleo.

I was really worried. Then I remembered Alex and the antlers. Maybe Alex had Cleo.

I stomped down the sidewalk to school. Cleo was my dog and I was going to get her back.

Alex, Ashley, and Adam were already in our classroom. Luckily, Mr. Parker wasn't there yet. I headed straight for the triplets and hollered, "Where's my dog?"

Ashley looked at me and shook her head.

Adam looked at me and shrugged.

Alex looked at me and smiled. "Look what I found in our basement." She held up a long piece of rope. "It will make a perfect reindeer harness for Cleo."

"Cleo is not your reindeer!" I yelled.

Alex stuck out her lip. "Why not?"

"Because she's missing!" I told her.

"Missing!" Adam and Ashley said together. Alex just dropped the rope and opened her mouth.

Barbara and Maria came up beside Alex. Barbara pointed to Alex and said, "What have you done with Sam's dog?"

Maria put her hands on her hips. "Have you lost his dog?"

Alex stomped her foot. "I haven't done anything to Cleo! I just wanted her to be a reindeer for a while."

"She didn't want to be a reindeer," I said.

Ashley shook her head. "Alex, this is all your fault."

Randy steered his wheelchair beside me.

"Poor Cleo," Randy said. "It's awfully cold outside." He didn't make me feel better.

Alex looked at me. Then her eyes got big and round. I knew what that meant. Alex was thinking. I worried about what she was thinking.

Alex snapped her fingers right in front of her nose. "I've got a plan to find Cleo."

7

Madder By
The Minute

Mr. Parker walked into the classroom. He grinned his big smile. I didn't feel like smiling back. I was too worried about Cleo. That's why I didn't cheer when Mr. Parker held up a sign with bright green and red letters: CHRISTMAS ART CONTEST.

"What does the winner get?" Alex called out.

Mr. Parker held up a huge candy bar.

Alex was so busy talking to everyone, she didn't get anything done. Alex whispered to everybody. Everybody but me. Pretty soon, Adam and Ashley were whispering, too.

I was getting madder by the minute. Being left out of a secret didn't make me feel any better about losing Cleo. I made a picture of Cleo. I gave her long brown hair and a big black nose. I even remembered to color the tip of her bushy tail white.

Mr. Parker rang the little bell on his desk. "Time's up," he told the class. "Who wants to show their art piece first?"

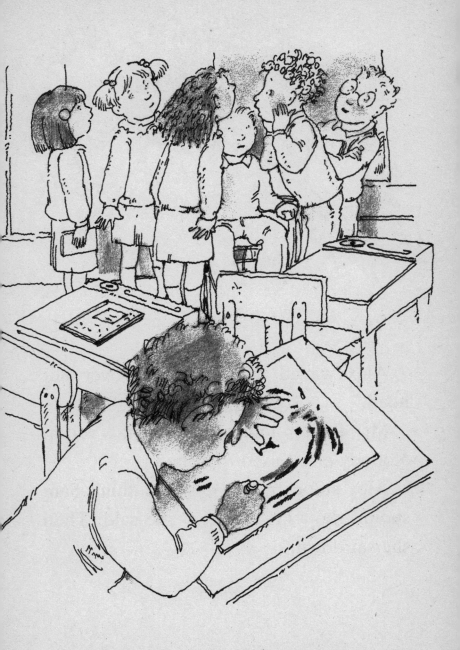

Alex waved her hand high over her
head.

Mr. Parker looked around the room.
Nobody else raised their hand.

Alex stood by her desk. "I think Sam
should show his picture," she said. Then
she sat down.

I didn't want to show my picture. I was too busy thinking about poor lost Cleo. But I held up my picture.

"Very nice," Mr. Parker said. "Who would like to go next?"

Everybody waited. I watched the second hand of the clock go around two times. Finally, Alex waved her hand in the air again.

Mr. Parker sighed. "Yes, Alex?"

"Nobody else finished," Alex told Mr. Parker, "so Sam wins the contest."

The rest of the class clapped their hands and Alex let out a whoop. Sometimes it's hard staying mad at Alex.

8

Marshmallows

I couldn't wait for school to end. When it did, I ran all the way home. I looked behind the garage and under the bushes. No Cleo. I didn't know where else to look so I sat down on the front porch. That's where the triplets found me.

Ashley patted me on the shoulder. "Cleo will come back," she said.

I sniffed. I didn't want to cry in front of the Tuckers, but I was beginning to feel like I might. "But what if she doesn't come home?" I asked.

I looked at Alex as she pulled a peppermint from her hair. She unwrapped it and popped it into her mouth. She was acting as if there was nothing to worry about.

"If you hadn't made Cleo into a reindeer she would still be here," I yelled at Alex. "Christmas is ruined and it's all your fault!"

"What are we going to do?" Ashley asked.

"Think about it," Alex said slowly. "What do dogs like the most?"

"Bones," Adam said.

"Besides that," Alex said.

"Tummy rubs," Ashley suggested.

Alex shook her head.

"Marshmallows," I blurted out.

Adam, Ashley, and Alex stared at me as if I'd sprouted reindeer antlers. "Well, Cleo likes marshmallows," I stammered.

Alex was thinking ag big and round. "Let's go find tha reindeer."

"Cleo is a dog!" I yelled.

I turned and ran home. I didn't care if I ever saw the Tucker Triplets again, especially Alex.

Ho! Ho!

When the doorbell rang, I didn't want to answer it. Dad told me I had to. It was Adam, Ashley, and Alex.

"Hi, Sam," Alex said cheerfully. "We have a plan."

"I don't care," I muttered.

"But it's a great plan," Adam told me.

He grabbed my arm and pulled me outside. "Come on."

. There was a sign on every tree, every pole, and every mailbox on our street. The signs all said the same thing:

Lost: Missing Reindeer Dog!

"Who made all these signs?" I asked.

Alex smiled. "Everybody did. That's what we did during the art contest."

"Every kid in the neighborhood is looking for Cleo," Ashley added.

"Mr. Parker, too," Adam said.

I felt bad about being so mad. Alex really was trying to find Cleo. After all, she liked Cleo almost as much as I did.

"Look!" Alex hollered.

A bunch of kids from school were in the Tucker's front yard. And Cleo!

"CLEO!" I hollered. I ran past the bicycles on the sidewalk. I raced past the stuffed scarecrow Santa decoration and the snowman family to squeeze Cleo's neck. She barked and licked my face.

"How did you find her?" I asked.

Barbara patted Alex on the back. "It was Alex's idea. We used marshmallows for bait. Cleo ate every one of them!"

I smiled at Alex. "You really are my best friend," I told her.

"But she still owes us our Secret Santa presents," Maria said.

"Presents?" Alex asked.

Alex looked at me. I looked at Adam. Adam looked at Ashley. Ashley looked at Cleo and sneezed.

Just then a big white car pulled up in front of the Tuckers' house. A lady with bright red lips came up to us.

"Congratulations, kids! You have won the prize for the best-decorated house," the lady said.

"We did?" Ashley asked.

"Yippee!" Alex, Adam, Ashley, and I shouted.

"What about our presents?" Maria asked again.

Alex snapped her fingers in front of her nose. "They're at Thelma's Toy Trunk!"

Everybody cheered again. I smiled and hugged Cleo. I already had what I wanted. Cleo — and three terribly good friends named Alex, Adam, and Ashley!